For Jo, my mum, with all my love.

Scholastic Children's Books,
Commonwealth House, 1~19 New Oxford Street,
London WC1A 1NU, UK
a division of Scholastic Ltd
London ~ New York ~ Toronto ~ Sydney ~ Auckland
Mexico City ~ New Delhi ~ Hong Kong

Published by Scholastic Ltd, 2000

Text and illustrations copyright © Debi Gliori, 2000

ISBN: 0 439 01372 0 Hardback

Printed in Belgium.
All rights reserved

2 4 6 8 10 9 7 5 3 1

Debi Gliori has asserted her moral right to be identified as the author and illustrator of this work,
in accordance with the Copyright, Designs and Patents Act, 1988.

Polar Bolero

Debi Gliori

SCHOLASTIC
PRESS

. . . and the moon's flying high

The story's beginning . . .

trailing fat clouds
across the night sky

and whispers, "Goodnight."

kisses me gently

In the dark comes
that someone
who goes HUG
in the night

So . . .
we're flying
back home
to where
somebody
cares, falling
into our
pillows, tightly
hugging our
bears.

over oceans
and mountains
across rivers
and streams

 as we Polar Bolero with
the owls and the bees

There is music and laughter drifting up from the trees

in peejays and slippers and some with bare feet.

And here is the hill
where the
wide~awake meet

through the deep summer grasses to the edge of the lawn, with the things that are LUMPS in the night.

past the gate

out the door

. . . and creep . . .